TODAY IS THE DAY

Nancy Riecken

Illustrated by Catherine Stock

Houghton Mifflin Company Boston 1996

For information about this and other Houghton Mifflin
trade and reference books and multimedia products,
visit The Bookstore at Houghton Mifflin on the World Wide
Web at http://www.hmco.com/trade/.

The text of this book is set in 15 point Janson
The illustrations are watercolor, reproduced in full color

TWP 10 9 8 7 6 5 4 3 2 1

Printed in Singapore

Library of Congress Cataloging-in-Publication Data
Riecken, Nancy.
Today is the day / Nancy Riecken : illustrated by Catherine Stock.
p. cm.
Summary: A young Mexican girl eagerly awaits her absent father's
return and hopes that he will bring enough money so that she can
walk to school in new shoes.
ISBN 0-395-73917-9
[1. Fathers and daughters—Fiction. 2. Mexico—Fiction.]
I. Stock, Catherine, ill.   II. Title.
PZ7.R4276To 1996
[E]—dc20   95-23927   CIP   AC

For Hermelindo, Virginia, Lydia, Saul, and Elias
—N.R.

For Dad—C.S.

"Wake up, Yara!" Yesenia jumped out of bed. "Today is the day!"

"Quiet down, Yese," her sister groaned. "I'm awake."

"But Papa could be here any minute." Yesenia laughed as she ran out the door.

Her skipping feet scattered the chicks in the yard. "Cheep! Chee-chee!" Their chirping blended with Yese's voice. "Today is the day! Papa's coming home today!"

The day he had left seemed so long ago. "Why did Papa leave?" Yese had asked.

"He has to find work," Mama replied. "There's been no rain for months, and corn won't grow in the dust."

"Can't he work here? Or in the city?"

Mama sighed. "There are no jobs, Yese. He has to go where the money is. And that's a long way from here."

"When will Papa come home?"

"He'll write. And maybe—just maybe—he'll bring enough for shoes and books for school."

"Oh, Mama! Can we really go to school this year?"

"I hope so. We'll see when your papa comes home."

Yesenia had remembered her mother's words for six long months. Finally Papa's letter arrived. She stared down the dirt road that led to the highway. Today a bus would stop where the roads met, and Papa would be on it. She could see him now, his face shaded by his tall white hat with the rattlesnake band.

"I'll meet you at the bus, Papa," Yesenia said out loud. "We'll walk home together. Won't everybody be glad to see us! And we'll all get new shoes—even Juanito!" She laughed at the thought of shoes on the baby's feet.

"Yese!" Mama called. "Breakfast is ready."

"Mama, what time will he be here? What bus will he be on? May I . . ."

Yara interrupted. "Papa's not coming back."

"Of course he's coming back!" Mama glared at Yara. "Don't be foolish! Eat your breakfast and don't say such nonsense."

Yesenia stared at her sister. Yara frowned back and shrugged. Yese didn't feel like eating anymore.

"How could you say that?" she asked later as they hung up the wash. "How can you think Papa wouldn't come home?"

"Look around, Yese. Other men leave and don't come back. What makes Papa any different?"

"He's our father!"

"So? Lucita Dominquez's father left three years ago. Martin Vasquez's father left when he was born. Antonio—"

"Not Papa! He'll come home. He said he would."

Yara sighed. "I want him to. But I'm just not going to hope."

"Papa loves us. He'll come back."

Yara hung the last cloth and turned away. Yesenia was so mad she wanted to throw something at her.

Instead she ran down the long road to the highway. "I'll show Yara! I'll bring Papa home." She reached the highway and waited under a mesquite tree, sure her father would be on the next bus.

But he wasn't. Yesenia walked up and down the road all morning, meeting each bus. People got on and off, but not Papa.

The sun grew high and hot. When Yesenia's stomach told her it was time to eat she finally went home.

"You ran off without finishing your work," Mama complained. "Where have you been?"

"Waiting for Papa. Oh, Mama, please let me go back. We'll come home together."

"While you've been playing I've been working," Yara grumbled.

"Please?"

Mama looked from Yese to the highway. "Go on, then. But tomorrow you'll be the one to sweep and wash and feed the animals."

"I will, Mama. Thank you!"

She was just in time to see the next bus pull to a stop. A tall man in a white hat got off. It's him! Yese's heart pounded with excitement. She waved wildly. As he waved back she could see his face.

It wasn't Papa. It was only Pedro Hernandez.

"What a surprise! It's not often my customers come out to meet me. I suppose I can sell you something right here. What's it going to be?"

Yesenia's mouth went dry. She wanted to scream, but only whispered, "No, sir. I thought you were my father. He's—"

"Ah! Children!" The peddler waved her aside. "I have customers to see."

Buses came and went. Some didn't even stop. Just before dark Yesenia turned and slowly stumbled back down the road. There was Mama standing in the doorway. "Come, my love," she said. "Sit down and rest."

"He didn't come," Yese cried.

Mama's hand rubbed a warm spot into her back. "Don't cry, Yese. Your papa will be home." She wrapped her arms around Yesenia and whispered a soft song in her ear. They sat together for a long time, watching the sun's last rays spread streaks across the sky. The first stars appeared high above them.

Mama stood up. "The last bus should be coming soon. Come on. Yara, you too. Let's all walk and wait together."

Taking turns carrying Juanito, they felt their way down the rutted road. The stars grew brighter as trucks sped by. Yesenia felt very small and held tight to her mother's hand.

There it was! The tall silver bus sped toward them. It was coming fast. Mama's grip tightened. Yese held her breath.

The bus went right on by.

As they watched its lights disappear, Mama dropped Yesenia's hand. Yese felt very glad now for the darkness.

The walk home was long. Yesenia shivered in the night air, but her face felt red-hot.

Suddenly a car sped up behind them, loud music blaring from inside. Everyone jumped off the road as it swerved past. The car jerked to a stop, spun around, and raced back toward the highway.

"Crazy driver!" Mama yelled. Then she saw Yara sprawled on the road.

"Yara!" Yesenia's heart sank to her feet.

"I'm okay, Mama. I . . . I tripped. But look . . . it's Papa!"
Papa ran toward them. "What are you doing out here?"
"We were waiting for you! Manuel, is it really you?
Where did you come from? The bus—"

"I was too late for the bus, so I got a ride—what a driver! But I couldn't wait another day. I was afraid you'd worry."

"Oh, Manuel." Mama sighed a long, long sigh.

"Welcome home!"

"Manuel Rodriguez is back!" neighbors called out as they walked through the village. "Good to see you again, Manuel!"

Yesenia walked proudly next to her father. "Are we rich now?" she asked.

He shook his head. "We have enough for a while. Money for what we need, anyway."

Yesenia had imagined walking to school in her new shoes. But better than that was having her father home.

"Please don't ever go away again."

"I can't promise that, Yese," Papa said quietly. "I don't know what the future will bring."

Yara wrapped her arm tightly around her father's waist. "I know one thing for sure, Papa," she said. "Yesenia trusted you, and she was right. You'll always come home again."